This Boxer Books paperback belongs to

........................................

**www.boxerbooks.com**

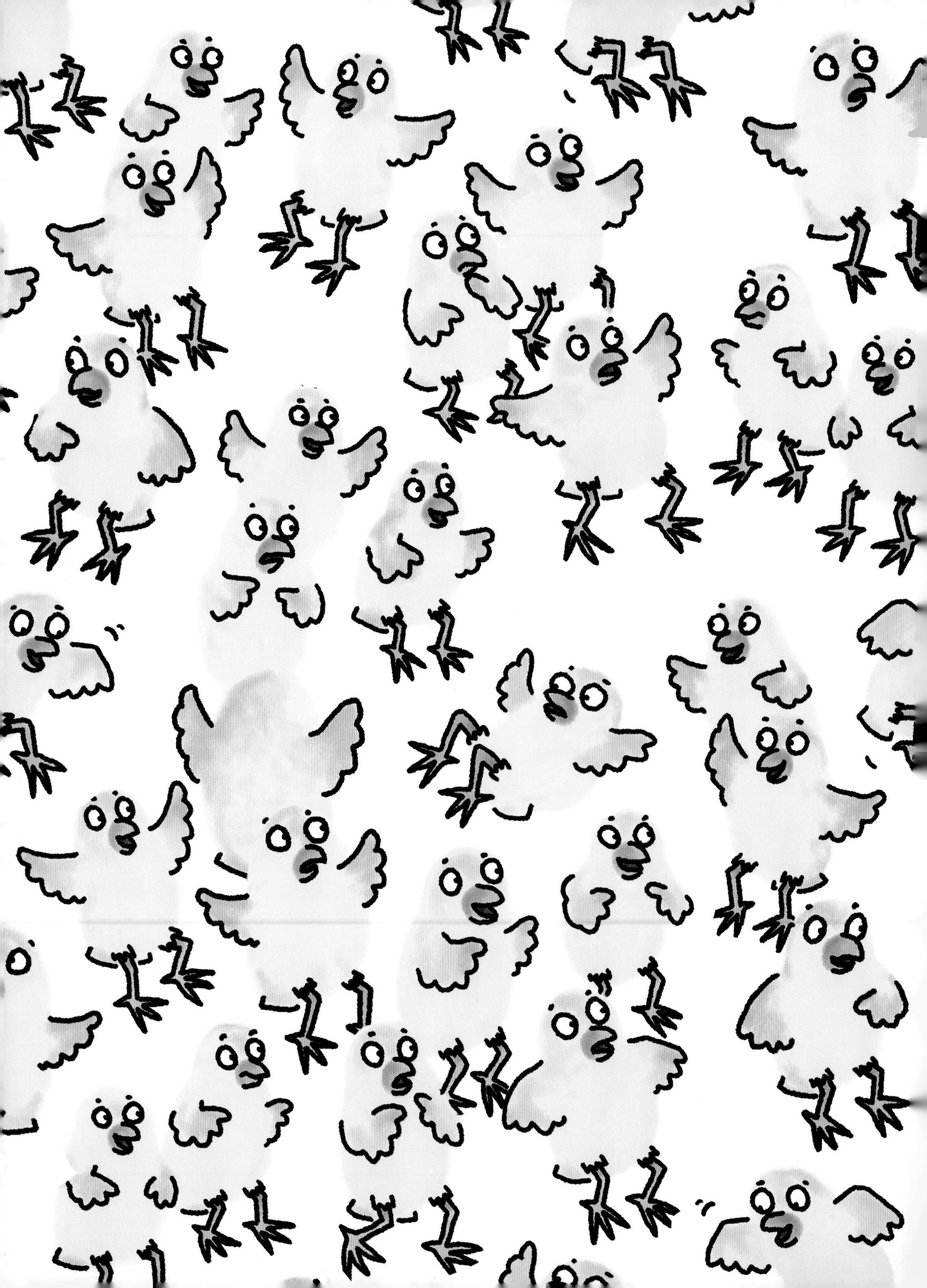

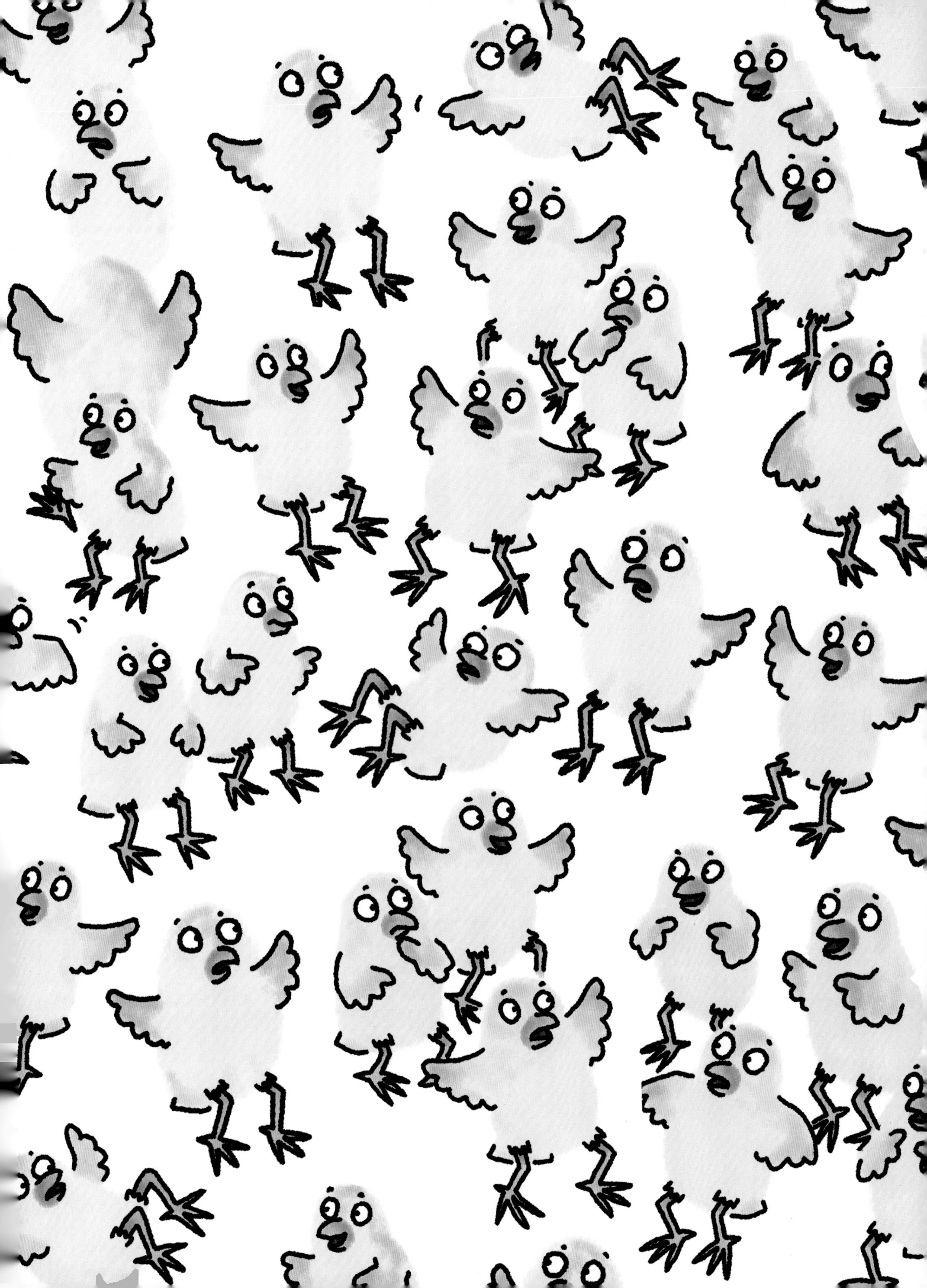

For Margaret Mahy, several of whose stories I had
the great pleasure of illustrating.
J.A.

First published in hardback in Great Britain in 2013 by Boxer Books Limited.
First published in paperback in Great Britain in 2013 by Boxer Books Limited.
www.boxerbooks.com

Text and illustrations copyright © 2013 Jonathan Allen

The illustrations were prepared digitally by the author
The text is set in Adobe Garamond Regular

ISBN 978-1-907967-85-6

1 3 5 7 9 10 8 6 4 2

Printed in China

All of our papers are sourced from managed forests and renewable resources.

# I'm not Reading!

## Jonathan Allen

Boxer Books

Baby Owl sat down with Owly
under a tree in the field by the farm.
He had his favourite book with him.

"Sit quietly, Owly," said Baby Owl,
"and I will read to you."

Baby Owl had just opened his book
when along came Tiny Chick.
"You're reading a story, Baby Owl!"
cried Tiny Chick. "May I listen too?"

"All right," said Baby Owl.
"But I'm not reading unless
you sit quietly like Owly."
"I will!" said Tiny Chick.

Before Baby Owl could begin,
along came Tiny Chick's two
brothers and two sisters.

"Baby Owl's reading a story!"
they cried. "Hooray!"
And they jumped
onto Baby Owl's lap!

"Hold on a minute!" protested Baby Owl.

"I'm not reading unless you all sit quietly like Owly and Tiny Chick!" "We will!" said Tiny Chick's brothers and sisters.

Baby Owl had just reached around them to open the book, when along came Tiny Chick's seven cousins.

"Baby Owl's reading a story!"
they cried. "Hooray!"
And they all piled onto
Baby Owl's lap.

"Wait a minute!" shouted Baby Owl.
"I'm not reading unless you all get off!"

# "WAAAAAAH!"

he cried.

But the chicks didn't hear him.

They were too busy pushing and shoving.

Just then, along came Tiny Chick's
school friends and their brothers
and sisters and cousins.

"What are you all doing?" they cried.
"Baby Owl's reading us a story!"
shouted Tiny Chick.

"Really?" asked one of the chicks. "Where *is* Baby Owl?"

"I'm here!" said Baby Owl
in a muffled voice.
"And I am NOT
reading, I'm being squashed! Help!"

Then along came Baby Owl's dad.
"Poor Baby Owl," he said,
lifting him up gently.
"What on earth were you doing
under there?"

"I was reading to Owly, then Tiny Chick came along, then his brothers and sisters and cousins, and then everybody else came too, and they all wanted me to read to them and they all sat on my lap and I got squashed! It's not fair!" said Baby Owl.

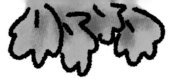

Along came Tiny Chick's mum. "Oh dear," she said. "I think Tiny and his friends are a little bit overexcited! They do so love being read to!"

"Well," said Baby Owl's dad,
"perhaps Baby Owl will read
to them if they promise not
to squash him."
"Yes, we promise," said Tiny Chick.
"Please read to us, Baby Owl!"
 "All right," said Baby Owl.

"Hooray!" cried all the chicks, and they jumped up onto Baby Owl's dad and Tiny Chick's mum.

Baby Owl laughed.
Then he opened his book
and read them all a story.

Later, Dad took Baby Owl home
and tucked him into his warm,
cosy bed.
"Shall I read you a story, Baby Owl?"
asked Dad.

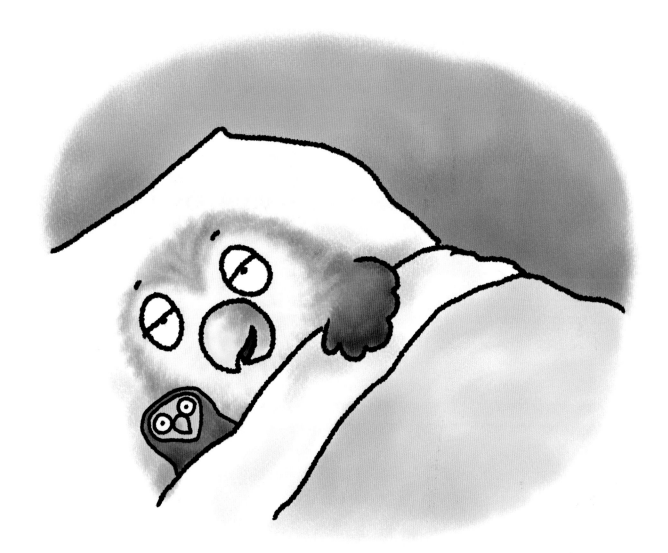

But Baby Owl was already falling asleep.
"Goodnight, Baby Owl," whispered Dad.

"Goodnight, Dad," mumbled Baby Owl.
"Goodnight, Owly."

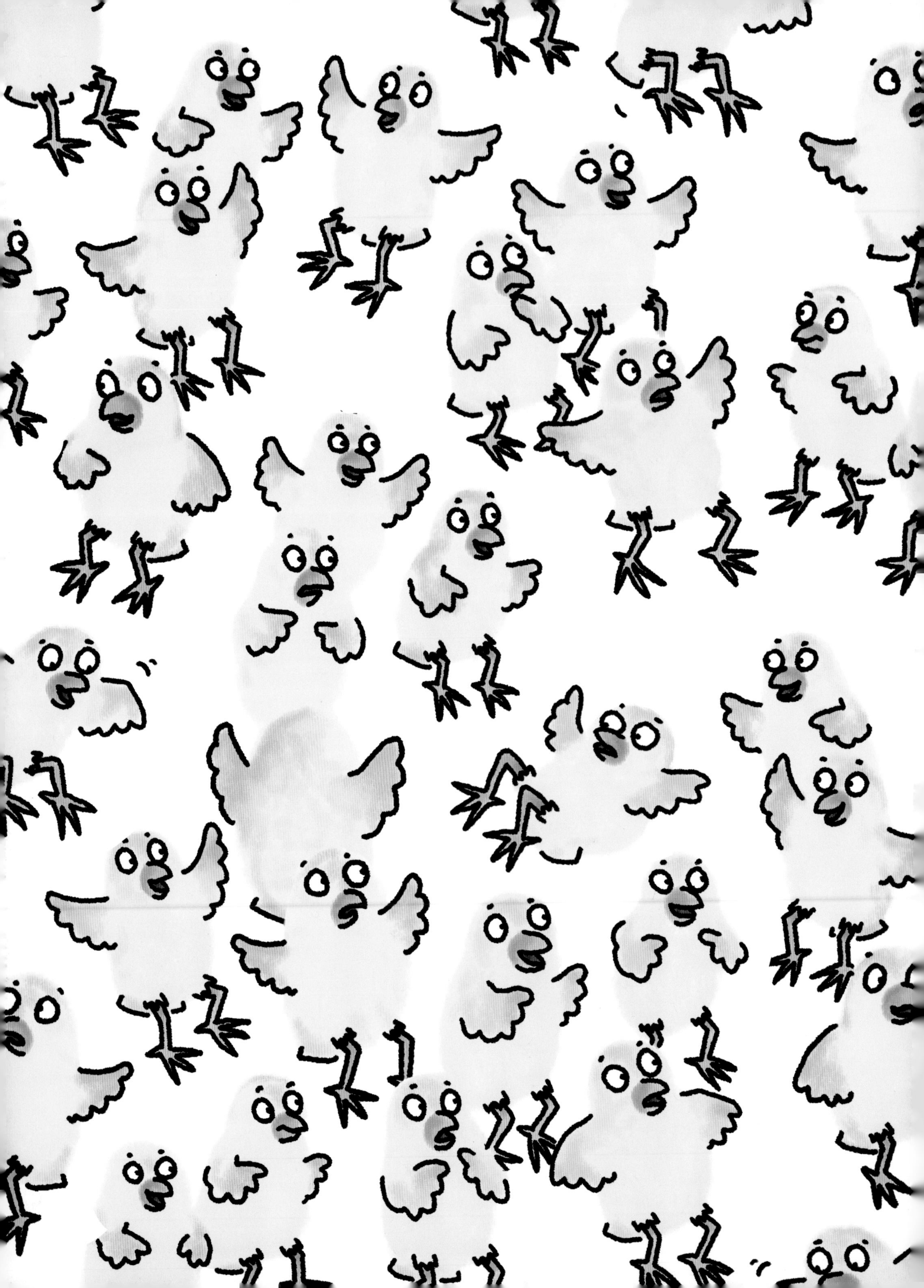

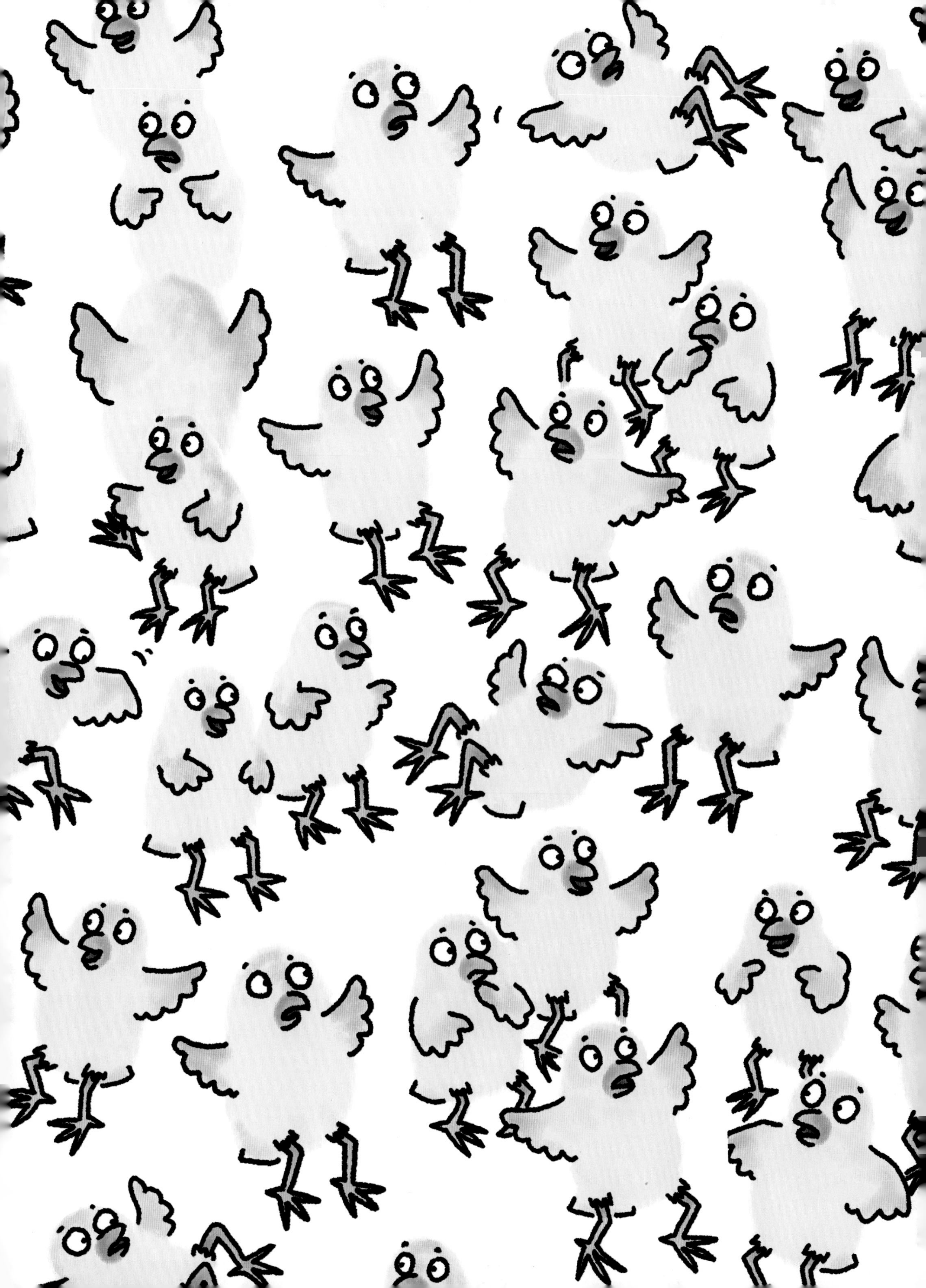

# More Baby Owl stories for you to enjoy by Jonathan Allen

'Made me laugh out loud . . . a delight.'
*The Observer*

' . . . the simplest of stories, but one that will bear frequent retellings.'
*Financial Times*

### I'm not Ready!
Baby Owl is going to pre-school – but guess what? He is not ready!
**Hardback** 3-6 years *280 mm x 215 mm, 32 pages* 978-1-907967-04-7 **£11.99**

### I'm not Cute!
Baby Owl decides to explore the woods, but all the animals he meets think that he is so cute and so fluffy, so they want to give him a big hug! But Baby Owl tells them, "I'm not cute!"
**Hardback** 3-6 years *280 mm x 215 mm, 32 pages* 978-0-95473-34-4 **£10.99**
**Paperback** 3-6 years *280 mm x 215 mm, 32 pages* 978-0-954737-38-2 **£6.99**
**Board Book** 0-3 years *180 mm x 140 mm, 26 pages* 978-1-905417-88-9 **£4.99**

### I'm not Scared!
Baby Owl is out for a moonlight stroll through the woods, but each animal he bumps into tells him not to be scared! Can Baby Owl convince them that owls are meant to be out at night?
**Hardback** 3-6 years *280 mm x 215 mm, 32 pages* 978-1-905417-27-8 **£10.99**
**Paperback** 3-6 years *280 mm x 215 mm, 32 pages* 978-1-905417-28-5 **£6.99**
**Board Book** 0-3 years *180 mm x 140 mm, 26 pages* 978-1-905417-87-2 **£4.99**

### I'm not Sleepy!
Baby Owl has stayed up all night, but he's definitely NOT sleepy. So why do all the other animals in the forest think it's past his bedtime?
**Paperback** 3-6 years *280 mm x 215 mm, 32 pages* 978-1-907967-06-1 **£6.99**
**Board Book** 0-3 years *180 mm x 140 mm, 26 pages* 978-1-907152-60-3 **£6.99**

### I'm not Santa!
Baby Owl is taking a Christmas Eve stroll though the woods with his sledge, when Baby Hare mistakes him for Santa. "I'm not Santa!" Baby Owl insists, and a comic Christmas tale unfolds.
**Paperback** 3-6 years *280 mm x 215 mm, 32 pages* 978-1-907152-52-8 **£6.99**
**Board Book** 0-3 years *180 mm x 140 mm, 26 pages* 978-1-906250-61-4 **£4.99**

The Art of Storytelling
www.boxerbooks.com